To Mark, Shelley, Nick, and Bob, with hopes that you
will always soar on the wings of imagination—Uncle Bob
For Maddog and Jake.—J.T.D.

Text ©1995 by Robert D. San Souci.
Illustrations ©1995 by Jan Thompson Dicks.
All rights reserved.
Book design by Marianne Mitten.
The illustrations in this book were rendered in acrylic
on watercolor paper.
Printed in Hong Kong.

Distributed in Canada by Raincoast Books
8680 Cambie Street, Vancouver, B.C. V6P 6M9

10 9 8 7 6 5 4 3 2 1

Chronicle Books
275 Fifth Street
San Francisco, California 94103

Library of Congress Cataloging-in-Publication Data

San Souci, Robert D.
The little seven-colored horse / written by Robert D.
San Souci ; illustrations by Jan Thompson Dicks.
        40p. 26.6 x 22.9 cm.
Summary: With perseverance and the help of a magical
horse, Juanito, the youngest son of a farmer, wins the
hand of the mayor's beautiful daughter.

ISBN 0-8118-0412-7

[1. Folklore—Southwest, New. 2. Folklore—Latin America.]
I. Dicks, Jan Thompson, ill. II. Title.
PZ8.1.S227Li   1995
398.2'0946'04529725—dc20   94-44525
                                    CIP
                                    AC

The Little Seven-Colored Horse

A Spanish American Folktale

Written by Robert D. San Souci
Illustrated by Jan Thompson Dicks

Chronicle Books • San Francisco

Once upon a time a farmer arose early in the morning to work in his cornfield. To his dismay, the *granjero* found that some beast had come by night and eaten many ears of corn. The husks of the *mazorcas* were scattered among trampled stalks.

"¡Ay! ¡Ay! ¡Ay!" the *granjero* cried. "We will be ruined!" His cries awoke his three sons. They gazed fearfully at the damage, wondering what sort of animal had ravaged their *maíz*.

The man told his eldest son, "Diego, guard our cornfield tonight."

But Diego fell asleep during his watch. The next morning, the *maizal* had been plundered just as before.

So the angry *granjero* told his second son, "Pedro, keep watch, and see that you do not fall asleep."

But this lazybones soon nodded off; once again, their *maíz* was eaten.

Finally the youngest brother, Juanito, or little Juan, said, "Let me keep watch. I will not let anything get our *maíz*."

His brothers laughed at him, saying, "How can you do what we could not?"

But Juanito took a length of *soga* and his guitar with him. He gathered the fattest *mazorcas* and piled them beneath a tree. Then he hid himself in its branches. With his rope close at hand, he strummed his guitar and sang softly to keep awake.

At midnight, a *caballito* galloped down from the sky into the cornfield. Juanito counted seven colors in the little horse's coat, but they never seemed to his eyes the same seven colors. They changed and changed again. The magical pony began to eat the *maíz* piled under the tree. Then Juan lassoed and captured it.

To the boy's amazement, the seven-colored horse said, "I beg you to let me go. If you do this, I promise that I will always help you if you find yourself in trouble. Just call:

Caballito de Siete Colores,
Once, I set you free;
Now, Little Seven-Colored Horse,
I ask you to help me.

And I will come to your aid."

"First," said Juanito, "you must promise not to eat my father's *maíz*."

"I give you my word," said the horse.

So Juanito loosened the rope, and the horse galloped into the sky and vanished.

When Juanito told his father and brothers what had happened, they laughed and said, "You fell asleep and dreamed."

But the next night and every night thereafter the *maíz* was left untouched. So the others realized that Juanito had told the truth.

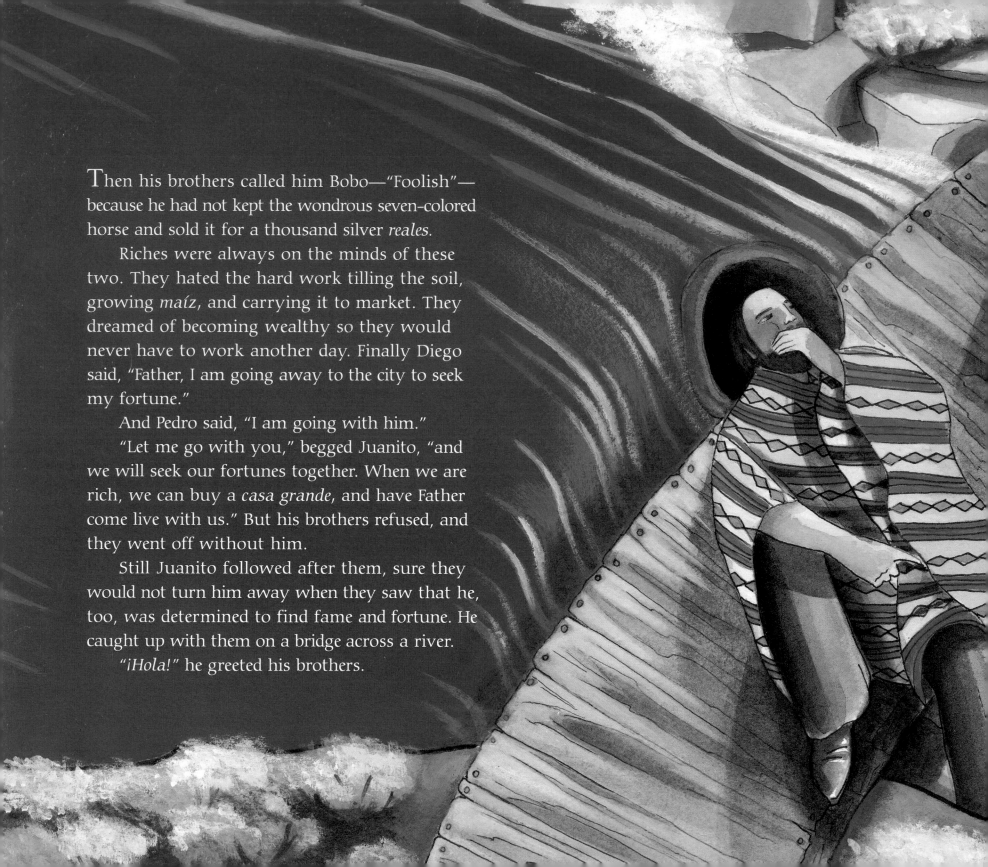

Then his brothers called him Bobo—"Foolish"—
because he had not kept the wondrous seven-colored
horse and sold it for a thousand silver *reales*.

Riches were always on the minds of these
two. They hated the hard work tilling the soil,
growing *maíz*, and carrying it to market. They
dreamed of becoming wealthy so they would
never have to work another day. Finally Diego
said, "Father, I am going away to the city to seek
my fortune."

And Pedro said, "I am going with him."

"Let me go with you," begged Juanito, "and
we will seek our fortunes together. When we are
rich, we can buy a *casa grande*, and have Father
come live with us." But his brothers refused, and
they went off without him.

Still Juanito followed after them, sure they
would not turn him away when they saw that he,
too, was determined to find fame and fortune. He
caught up with them on a bridge across a river.

"*¡Hola!*" he greeted his brothers.

"¡*Hola!*" responded Diego, giving Pedro a wink. Then Diego said, "Look, Juanito! There is something in the water!"

"*Sí,*" Pedro agreed, peering into the river. "Is it gold?"

But when Juanito bent down to look, his brothers pushed him into the swift-flowing stream.

"¡*Adiós, pescadito!*" Diego called.

"Goodbye, little fish!" echoed Pedro.

Laughing and clapping each other on the back, they hurried off, giving not a single thought to poor Juanito, who was swept along by the river.

Barely staying afloat, Juanito clutched at every rock until he managed to grab hold of a tooth of rock in midstream. Too tired to swim to shore, he almost gave up hope. Then he remembered what the magical horse had told him. So he called out:

> Caballito de Siete Colores,
> *Once, I set you free;*
> *Now, Little Seven-Colored Horse,*
> *I ask you to help me.*

Instantly the horse galloped down out of the sky. He raced atop the river as though the rushing water were as solid as the king's highway. When he reached Juanito, the boy climbed onto the pony's bare back, clinging to his mane.

"Where shall I take you?" asked the horse.

"To the city," said Juanito, "to seek my fortune."

"Very well," said the seven-colored horse. As they flew south and east, Juanito suddenly caught a floating dark blue *pluma*, tipped with silver.

"Toss that feather away," said the horse, "or it will bring you bad luck."

But Juanito said, "Surely something this pretty can only bring me good luck." And he stuck the jaunty *pluma* in his cap.

Soon Juanito saw the city beneath them. The horse flew down to the ground. When the boy had dismounted, the pony returned to the clouds. Juanito went to an inn, where he asked the innkeeper, "Might there be a job for me here?"

 The innkeeper hired Juanito to sweep the patio and fetch water and wash dishes. In return, he gave Juanito a bed and some *frijoles* and *arroz*.

As he ate his beans and rice, Juanito heard two serving girls talking about María, the beautiful daughter of the city's *alcalde*, Don José Éscobar. The girl had so many suitors, they said, that she was unable to choose among them. So she had decided to wed the man who won the *sortijas*, the tournament of rings. The contest was to be held on Sunday after mass; all unmarried men in the town, including the *hidalgos*, each the son of a wealthy *don*, would compete for María's hand.

On Sunday, Juanito asked to go and watch the tournament. But the innkeeper said, "First you must finish all your chores." Though there was work enough for two, Juanito swept and scrubbed and polished so that he finished in next to no time. Then he called:

> Caballito de Siete Colores,
> *Once, I set you free;*
> *Now, Little Seven-Colored Horse,*
> *I ask you to help me.*

This time the horse came with a saddle and reins of the finest leather, inlaid with gold and silver. Tied in a bundle to the silver pommel was a dark-blue velvet jacket, trousers with silver buttons and embroidery, suede boots decorated with peacock-blue silk thread, and a magnificent *sombrero*.

Juanito climbed upon the back of the little seven-colored horse.

Off they trotted to the plaza, where a crowd had gathered to watch the young men try to win the hand of María, the mayor's daughter.

The instant Juanito saw her all dressed in white, walking beside her father, she captured his heart. When she was seated under an awning, the *alcalde* signalled for the contest to begin.

Astride the seven-colored horse, Juanito looked more dashing than any other rider. María spotted him at once, and asked her father, "Who is the *hidalgo* on the fanciful horse?"

But her father did not know.

Now Juanito's brothers, Diego and Pedro, were also competing for María's hand. Recognizing his brother, Diego said, "Juanito *Bobo*, what are you doing here on an underfed mount that does not even know what color a proper horse should be?"

Juanito sat up proudly in his saddle and said, "Hold your laughter until the contest is over."

"We will, *Bobo*," sneered Pedro. "Then we will laugh even louder."

The tournament began as the first riders took off. Holding their pommels with one hand, they used lances to try to catch rings of colored ribbon that hung above the length of the racecourse.

Many riders—including Juanito's brothers—came near to winning. But in the last race, to the crowd's cheers, Juanito snared all the rings.

Juanito rode to María, dismounted, removed his *sombrero*, and knelt before her, holding out his lance with its rainbow of rings. "Doña María, I present this to you; and I present to your father my claim for your hand in marriage."

María smiled warmly and fluttered her fan prettily. But before the *alcalde* could reply, Pedro and Diego pushed through the crowd. They were furious that Juanito had won the contest.

"Don José," said Diego, bowing low, "Do you see the elegant *pluma* in our brother's hat? Only this morning, Juanito vowed that if he won the race, he would fetch the bird from which it came and give it to your daughter as a gift."

"Is this true?" asked the *alcalde*.

Before Juanito could deny it, Pedro said, "*¡Sí!* I heard him say this very thing."

Then María said, "Would you do this for me?"

Helpless before her dark eyes and bright smile, Juanito could only say, "Whatever you wish."

Soon after this, Juanito set out toward the south, riding the little seven-colored horse. Some distance from the city, the horse said, "See, Juanito? I told you that *pluma* would bring bad luck. Now we face a long, dangerous search to find that bird."

"I am sorry, *amigo*," the boy said, stroking the horse's mane. "I should have listened. I won't have you risk yourself because of my foolishness. Go! I will seek the bird on my own."

"Nonsense," said the horse. "Friends don't desert friends. You have learned your lesson, so let's be off!"

They flew over deserts of hot white sand, snowcapped blue mountains, and forests a thousand shades of green that stretched as far as Juanito could see.

At last they came to a *laguna*, whose waters and tree-lined shores were thronged with birds of every size and color: parrots, macaws, toucans, flamingos, and countless others.

As they flew down toward the lagoon, the birds rose up in waves of color, screeching and slashing at them with beaks and talons as sharp as daggers.

"The bird you seek is king of these creatures. Use this sword to defend yourself," said the horse. Juanito found a golden sword fastened to the pommel of his saddle. With it, he defended them from the angry birds. After a fierce battle, the winged army flew off. Then the horse carried Juanito to the southernmost shore of the *laguna*.

The moment his hoofs touched the ground, the sword in Juanito's hand became a golden cage. Nearby, Juanito saw a marvelous bird, its deep blue feathers tipped with silver. It was so ancient it could no longer fly. Juanito felt such pity, he could not touch it.

But the bird said, "I am old and weary, and long to cross the skies one last time. Take me with you, and let me see the world from above once more."

Gently Juanito set the bird in the cage. Then horse and rider began their long journey home.

Now while Juanito was away, Diego and Pedro (who were to be María's brothers-in-law) were granted important positions in the household of the *alcalde*. There they learned that years before, the King of Spain had sent a priceless golden ring, studded with diamonds, emeralds, and rubies, to Don José in thanks for his loyal service to the crown. But the ship that carried the ring had been sunk by a storm before reaching shore.

The moment that Juanito presented the wondrous bird to his beloved María, Diego and Pedro took the *alcalde* aside.

"Don José," said Diego, "our brother has promised us that he will fetch you the golden ring that was lost at sea."

Then Pedro added, "He hopes that you will let him bestow it on your lovely daughter as a *memoria*."

The delighted *alcalde* announced that Juanito had promised to recover the lost ring as an engagement present for María.

Snared by his brothers' lies, Juanito agreed to the seemingly impossible task.

Alone, Juanito walked to the shore and gazed hopelessly over the waves. Though he felt even the little horse could not help him this time, he called:

> Caballito de Siete Colores,
> *Once, I set you free;*
> *Now, Little Seven-Colored Horse,*
> *I ask you to help me.*

Soon the loyal steed raced down from the sky. When Juanito had explained the challenge set for him, the horse said, "Hold fast to the pommel and don't let go for an instant, or you will drown."

Then the horse raced into the sea. As the waves closed over his head, Juanito clung to the silver pommel with both hands. To his surprise, he found that he could breathe the water as easily as air.

The seven-colored horse carried him through waving green forests of *algas marinas* and living curtains of bright-colored *peces* that parted before him. Far ahead, in the blue-black water, Juanito saw a golden gleam, no bigger than the head of a pin.

"That is the ring," the horse told him, "but you will need even more skill than you showed at the tournament of rings to snatch it from the creature that guards it."

Juanito could see that the gleaming spot lay in the shadows of a sunken ship. On either side, the wooden ribs curved up like the walls of a church.

At first, it seemed that the golden ring rested on a small hill. Then, to his horror, Juanito saw that the hill was actually a giant *langosta*. The golden ring was caught on one antenna of the monstrous lobster.

As soon as horse and rider were close enough, the *langosta* began snapping its saw-toothed *pinzas* at them. The deadly claws went *snick-snap, snick-snap*. The horse circled the creature, darting close then backing off, leaping over just out of reach of the huge pinchers.

"Use one hand to seize the ring," said the horse. "But hold the pommel with the other, or you will drown."

Again and again, Juanito tried to capture the prize. But the fearsome sea-beast moved so quickly and used its *pinzas* so skillfully, that—*snick-snap*—it nipped Juanito's arms and legs many times.

Growing weary, Juanito said to the little horse, "Draw out the monster one last time. I have a final plan."

Obediently, the horse charged at the creature, then retreated. *Snick-snap*, went the *pinzas* of the *langosta* as it rushed forward. *Snick-snap. Snick-snap.*

Suddenly, Juanito let go of the pommel. The monster, all its attention on the little seven-colored horse, did not move quickly enough as Juanito arced above it, tugged free the golden ring, and swam for the surface.

But the moment Juanito let go of the pommel, his lungs filled with water. Still he swam up and up, clutching the ring, even as felt himself drowning.

Then the little seven-colored horse was beside him. Juanito grabbed the pommel with his free hand. Instantly, he could breathe.

The two galloped across the waves, beyond the shore to the house of the *alcalde*. There, Juanito presented the gold *memoria* to his beloved María.

Diego and Pedro glared at their brother as they made their way toward the *alcalde* with more mischief in mind. But Juanito quickly said, "Don José, my brothers told me that they wish to carry your greetings to the King of Spain, and share the happy news of the ring's recovery."

"*¡Bueno!*" cried the *alcalde*, embracing Diego and Pedro, "You set sail for Spain tomorrow morning."

The brothers spent half the voyage blaming each other for what had happened. After that, they decided that they were destined to find their fame and fortune at the Spanish court.

What befell them, history does not record. It is enough to know that they never returned to trouble Juanito and María, who were married and lived quite happily. They invited Juanito's father to come and live with them, and he became the closest friend of the *alcalde*.

The couple built the little seven-colored horse a splendid stable, and he remained their loyal companion for the rest of their days.

Colorín colorado;
Que este cuento
Se ha acabado.

And *colorín* so red;
This tale
Is said. *

* This is a traditional formula ending for a tale. The translators in both *Mexican Folktales from the Borderland* [see notes] and *Folktales of Mexico* [see notes also] indicate that *colorín* is not translated. *Colorín* indicates shiny red seeds used by water carriers in Mexico to count the number of deliveries to a particular house. A note in *Folktales of Mexico* suggests, "Use of the seeds as counters may be the reason for the presence of the *colorín* as part of the formal close of a story." It falls into the same pattern of "nonsense" formulas as the Caribbean," I step on a thing/And the thing bends/And that's the way my story ends," or such European closings as this, from one tale by the Brother's Grimm: "There once was a mouse, but he's gone,/and now my tale is done."

GLOSSARY

—◇—

Adiós (ah-dee-OHS): Goodbye

Alcalde (al-KAL-day): Mayor

Algas marinas (AHL-gahs mah-REE-nahs): Seaweed

Amigo (ah-MEE-goh): Friend

Antena (an-TAY-nah): Antenna; feeler

Arroz (ah-RROHS): Rice

¡Ay! (eye): Oh, dear!

Bobo (BOH-boh): Foolish

Caballito (cah-bah-YEE-toh): Little horse; small horse; pony

Casa grande (CAH-sah GRAHN-deh): Big house; mansion

Colores (koh-LOH-rehs): Colors

Colorín (koh-loh-REEN): Bright, shiny color

Cuento (KWEN-toh): Story, tale

Don (dohn): Sir; gentleman

Doña (DON-nyah): Lady; gentlewoman

Frijoles (free-HOH-lays): Beans; refried beans

Granjero (gran-HAY-roh): Farmer

Hidalgo (ay-DAHL-goh): Son of an important person

Hola (OH-lah): Hello

Laguna (lah-GOO-nah): Lagoon; shallow lake

Langosta (lahn-GOHS-tah): Lobster

Maíz (mah-EES): Corn

Maizal (mah-ee-SAL): Cornfield

Mazorca (mah-SOR-kah): Ear of corn

Memoria (may-MOH-ray-ah): Engagement present; memento

Pescadito (pehs-kah-DEE-toh): Fish

Peces (PAY-says): (Live) fish

Pinzas (PEEN-sahs): Pinchers; claws; nippers

Pluma (PLOO-mah): Feather

Que (keh): That

Reales (ray-AHL-ays): Coins

Se ha acabado (say ah ah-kah-BAH-doh): Is said; is finished; is completed

¡Sí! (see): Yes!

Siete (see-EH-teh): Seven

Soga (SOH-ga): Rope; cord; halter

Sombrero (sohm-BREH-roh): Broad-brimmed hat

Sortijas (sohr-TEE-hahs): Rings woven of ribbons; by extension, a tournament of rings

NOTES ON SOURCES AND SETTINGS

———◇———

The story of the wondrous seven-colored horse is popular throughout the Spanish-speaking world. I have drawn off numerous versions for this retelling, including two versions recorded in *Folk-Lore from the Dominican Republic*, which were translated from the Spanish for me by my friend J. Luís Jauregui. Other versions consulted include several in *Spanish Folk-Tales from New Mexico* by José Manuel Espinosa and *Mexican Folktales from the Borderland* [Texas/New Mexico/Mexico] by Riley Aiken, and *Folktales of Mexico*, edited and translated by Americo Paredes. I also located four versions from Puerto Rico which provided further insights into the story.

The root story originally came to the Americas from Spain, but variants of the tale can be found throughout Europe. One especially useful one was "Imperishable," in *Fairy Tales of the Slav Peasants and Herdsmen*, from the French of Alexander Chodsko, translated and illustrated by Emily J. Harding (1896). Other variants can be found in Russia and Israel.

Numerous background readings provided details of life in colonial Spanish America. Particularly helpful were: *Literary Folklore of the Hispanic Southwest*, gathered and interpreted by Aurora Lucero-White Lea; *Charro: Mexican Horseman*, by James Norman; and *Sun, Sand, and Steel: Costumes and Equipment of the Spanish/Mexican Southwest*, written and illustrated by Glen Dines.

The setting of the farm (*granja*) would be somewhere in the region of Texas-New Mexico/northern Mexico; the city would be on the Gulf of Mexico; the journey to the secret lagoon would carry horse and rider deep into South America. The time would be the later Spanish colonial period: from the late 1700s through the very early 1800s.